Copyright © 2021 by Abby Knox

All rights reserved.

No part of this book may be reproduced in any form or by any electronic or mechanical means, including information storage and retrieval systems, without written permission from the author, except for the use of brief quotations in a book review.

Publisher's Note: This is a work of fiction. Names, characters, places, and incidents are a product of the author's imagination. Locales and public names are sometimes used for atmospheric purposes. Any resemblance to actual people, living or dead, or to businesses, companies, events, institutions, or locales is coincidental.

Edited by Aquila Editing

Cover Designer: Cover Girl Design

ABBY KNOX

Summary

Island pilot Austin meets a lot of interesting people. But he's never met anyone quite like Sierra. When he learns this is her one final vacation before taking on the responsibilities of mommy-hood, he finds himself wishing for daddy-hood for the first time in his life. He's never considered settling down, but when he looks into her eyes, he can't imagine not starting a family.

Sierra has wanted a baby her entire life, but life has not yet provided a partner to make that happen. In advance of taking matters into her own hands with the help of fertility doctors, she leaves town for one last wild adventure with her best friend. When the rugged island pilot hears about Sierra's plans, he makes her an outrageous offer. It's absolutely ridiculous to even consider such a thing ... or is it?

Chapter One

Austin

THE TWO WOMEN approaching my aircraft look like best friends who just got away with the heist of the century.

The tall one with long braided hair covers her mouth, laughing breathlessly at a story the shorter one is telling. The five-foot-two sun-kissed blonde wears a loose potato-sack of a dress that hides a small frame. "…so I told him, 'I don't know where she is. But if she's not at the church on her wedding day, then that might be a clue she's not going to participate in your sham of a wedding. Maybe by the time she re-emerges, your head will have re-emerged from your ass, Mr. Pierce.'

The tall brunette shakes her head. "This story is never going to get old."

I re-check my flight manifest: Sierra Kennedy and Jax Pierce.

The two of them raise their matching bride-and-groom

tumblers, clinking them together in an impromptu toast. Curious.

"To ancient history," says the sun-kissed blonde.

"To new beginnings!" exclaims the tall one.

I've flown every type of visitor from island to island in this tiny fringe in the South Pacific. Gangsters, movie stars, politicians, and sketchy financiers flock to this remote stretch of paradise. The things I've overheard would fill a book. I could write it, but nobody would believe it. Or I could get myself killed for spilling secrets.

The women in front of me introduce themselves, and I learn the tall one—presumably the subject of the runaway bride story—is Jax. The short blonde who piques my interest is Sierra. Of course, she is. She's earthy, curvy, sun-kissed, and has the sweetest freckles I've ever seen dotting her nose.

A stiff sea breeze blows the straw hat off the petite blonde, whose sheer dress whips upwards at the same time. For the briefest of seconds, I think I see undies. However, I soon realize I'm looking at a navy blue polka dotted string bikini bottoms. The strings hanging down accent a set of curvy hips, the kind of hips that trigger a whole lot of inappropriate thoughts. I know it's unprofessional to let my mind wander while staring at a female passenger, but I can't help it. The image is there before I can think to shut it down. And what I'm thinking about is how much I'd love to hold onto those sweet hips while she tells me the whole story of the runaway bride, starting from the beginning. I want to hear her say more, especially while I'm tugging away at those strings. Maybe I'd even let her finish the story before those bottoms fall to the floor.

But that's not going to happen. I'm not interested in getting involved with a resort guest. Those people don't stick around for long. And me? I'm a long-haul guy. Not interested in flings. Not even with this charming little spit-fire who's triggering thoughts that make my cock twitch.

Sierra yelps and starts to run after her hat, slightly stumbling in her tall espadrilles. But I'm faster. When I place the hat back on her head, and our eyes meet, I nod and give her a tight smile, trying to keep a hold on my emotions, hoping like hell she doesn't see the caged animal that she's awakened with that sweet smile. She blinks up at me, and I can see she's someone special. Surely, someone back home loves her.

But I can look.

Sierra blushes, and her eyes dart down as she digs through her bag looking for something, then hands me an envelope of bills. "Before I forget," she says, smiling shyly.

I don't know what she's doing at first: I'm too caught up in her lips, curved up slightly. Her suntanned, freckled cheeks turn a pretty shade of pink as I stare down at her.

I frown at the stack of bills in her hand and shake my head. "No tips, ma'am. I'm already paid as part of your all-inclusive trip package," I explain.

Her friend turns to her. "See? I told you that's how it works."

"But surely," Sierra begins to insist, shaking the envelope at me.

"No, thank you," I tell her, placing my hands over hers. The warmth that transfers from her hands to mine pushes at my resolve.

The instant connection could burn out one of my aircraft engines by proximity. "I won't take money from you. But I will need your phone number."

A pink blotch creeps across Sierra's collarbones.

"Uh…" She laughs, and I realize what I've just said could be taken the wrong way.

Jax exclaims, "Oh! So you can let us know when the

plane is ready to take us back to the main island two weeks from today. Obviously. The travel agent said something about how you set your own schedule."

Sierra's eyes travel across my shoulders, and I shift my weight, steeling myself, willing my traitorous cock to settle down.

"Exactly." I keep my eyes locked on Jax, needing to avoid Sierra's expectant gaze. Those curious eyes and parted lips on the little blonde are a trap.

Sierra stuffs the bills back in her purse and uses her phone to drop her contact info to my phone in an exchange that dares me not to look at her face, her hair, the soft skin of her hands. I don't want to stare. My mind is made up.

The trouble is that every other part of my body is also made up, directly opposing my rational mind.

Chapter Two

Sierra

It's a good thing the pilot wears a headset and can't hear a word that Jax and I are saying to each other. We sound like drunk idiots.

Along with the slightly slurred speech thanks to the margaritas that the airport bartender was so kind to pour into our tumblers, the subject matter is not something I want to share with strangers.

We've hashed and rehashed the topic of her narrow escape from an arranged marriage, and now I've no escape from what Jax wants to talk about. Unless I want to skydive out of this Cessna. I might just try it.

When Jax asked me to join her on her would-be honeymoon to The Pearl Crescent islands, I suggested we leave a week early and spend some time in the city on Pearl Island before hitting the resort on Little Loggerhead. After doing some research, I learned the big island's city center has excellent shopping, a university, good hospitals, and a world-renowned fertility clinic. I decided I can do what I need to do here just as well as anywhere else. My family is not excited about my decision to have a baby on my own. So I might as well do it in paradise, away from their judging eyes.

My parents don't seem to realize that I'm almost 30 and that I've wanted a baby my entire life. As a child, there was nothing I wanted to play with more than baby dolls, toy strollers, and tiny cribs. Now that I'm an adult, I'm more of an adventurer than a homebody, but the idea of having a baby has never left me. When I close my eyes, I see me and a little girl or boy, holding hands, walking to the park. A suitable partner has never revealed himself to me, and that's okay. I've got the time, resources, and the will to raise a baby on my own.

"I can't believe this is our last girls' trip. Do you really have to go through with the insemination? I mean, a baby? It's so…so…final!"

Jax has a flair for the dramatic.

I laugh at her. "My life isn't going to be over just because I'm going to have a baby, you know."

She lolls her head back and wags it back and forth as if she can't believe what she's hearing.

"Babe," she counters. "Sierra…my best friend…a mom…I just…wow."

I smirk and sip from my tumbler. "Solid argument, but I'm going to do it."

"But why?"

I love my Jax, but having a baby is not the end of the world.

"Because," I answer her, "I've always wanted a baby. I have always felt it in my soul. Somehow I've always known I was built for it. And, I'm turning thirty next week, and I always said that if I wasn't married and pregnant by thirty, that I would go it on my own. And I want to have one big adventure with my best friend before I'm preggers."

A loud belch erupts from Jax's throat, and the pilot glances at us over his shoulder. "Tossing your cookies in my plane is one of those things not covered in your all-inclusive package."

Jax points and laughs at our pilot's comment. "You're funny." She turns to me and mouths, "and hot A.F."

My eyes roll so hard they might stay that way. "Jax. Oh my god."

Arching an eyebrow, she leans forward and places a hand on my knee. "Okay. Listen." Her classic move when she's tipsy is to remind a person to listen when they are, indeed, already listening. She's so cute right now I could hug her. "I promise not to bug you anymore about your future relationship with a turkey baster if you promise that on this trip, you'll at least consider getting knocked up by a romantic, dashing stranger."

She's officially drunk now. And bonkers.

I cluck at her. "In what universe does a stranger getting me pregnant make things less complicated?"

Jax chokes on her margarita, and I take the tumbler out of her hands. She's had enough until we land, I think. "It doesn't! But it sure is more fun, and romantic, and adventurous. Not to mention you'll have an amazing story to remember."

"If by adventurous, you mean a game of 'Will I or Won't I Contract Herpes on my All-Inclusive Island Vacation?' Then, sure. What a romantic adventure."

"Better than a sterile fertility clinic involving rubber gloves and refrigerated Harvard sperm!"

Now I'm choking. "The donor is a Johns Hopkins University professor, thank you very much," I correct her.

She glowers at me. "Whatever. Just promise me you'll keep your options open."

I stare back at Jax and entertain the prospect of her not harassing me every five minutes to keep an open mind. So, I lie. "Of course I will. But think of it this way, whichever way I get pregnant, you get to be the cool aunt."

My best friend twirls her long, thick braid and purses her lips thoughtfully. "Mm. I've always thought of myself as the crazy aunt."

Nodding, I christen her Crazy Aunt Jax, and I hand her the tumbler so we can make a toast.

"To Sierra's Babymoon!"

"To my Babymoon!"

The plane banks left, and I see it. Little Loggerhead Island: An oblong landmass of dense jungle, hugging a dormant volcano on one end and the exclusive Cerulean Resort and Spa on the other end. Pristine white sand beaches circle the entirety of the island. The turquoise water is so clear that I can see the line of coral reefs from the shore for miles out to sea. Beyond the private island is a half-moon-shaped line of smaller islands and keys, as well as a sprinkling of landmasses that amount to little more than sandbars with a few rocks and dense trees.

Jax gasps and points out the window to a small green strip of land to the south of Little Loggerhead. "There's Temple Island. That's where we're doing donkey yoga in the morning. Accessible by kayak only," Jax reports in her spokesperson's voice.

"Oh, no, thank you very much. I'll be sipping rum with my feet in the sand at that time."

Jax cocks her head. "It's at nine a.m."

"Listen. Babymoon is for making bad choices one last time before I have to be responsible for another human. Yoga does not fit the mission of Babymoon."

"What about parasailing? And cliff diving? And the mountain bike sunset ride on Captain Pete's Cove?"

I tap my finger to my lip and go down the list. "Maybe. Possibly. And only if I'm being pulled on the bike behind one of those pedicab things."

"They don't have those here."

The engine noise grows by several decibels on our descent, and the treetops are so close now I grip my seat cushion, fearing that we might crash into a mountain and I'll either die in the wreckage or by alligator attack. Wait, do they have alligators here? Local flora and fauna are things I hadn't bothered to look up.

From this angle, I don't see the tiny airstrip just on the other side of the tree line. When it comes into view, I let out a breath.

"In that case," I say brightly, "I'll be getting a spa treatment at sunset. Sorry, sunset bike tour."

"Every night?"

"No. Other nights, I'll be out living up to my end of our agreement. Scoping out a donor of hot island jizz rather than cold, clinical, professor jizz. Just like you suggested." I give her a wink to let her know I'll be doing no such thing—what a ridiculous idea.

Jax covers her mouth while she cackles. "Of the two of us, you are the crazy aunt."

I smile and watch the back of our pilot's head and pray to whatever god they worship in The Pearl Crescent islands that he hasn't heard a word of what we've been saying.

Chapter Three

Austin

"I THOUGHT YOU WERE ON VACATION."

Sam, the bartender, rightly wonders what I'm still doing here on Little Loggerhead Island.

I gesture to the surf shop tee-shirt and Bermuda shorts I'm wearing. "Don't I look like a tourist?"

He chuckles. "Sure do. I figured you'd be long gone by now."

I shrug. "I was going to go to Vegas and see some buddies from my unit, but last time I did that, it was a lot of kids and babies and talk about school. If I go now, they'll all be talking about college and shit. And then there's me. No wife. No kids. Not much to talk about."

Sam pops open a second beer and takes my empty. "I can see that. Maybe it's time to take the plunge yourself."

I smile ruefully and ignore that suggestion. "You know, I'm thinking of staying here and enjoying the islands off duty."

I've got two weeks of vacation saved up, and I could spend the money I've saved to go elsewhere and get away from the islands where I work every day. I could drink a beer anywhere in the world besides here on the pier, wearing out my usual barstool at the Mumbling Ahab with the boat captains and deckhands. I sip my beer and admire the sunset over the water, watching groups of guests and lovers stroll by hand in hand.

That's when I spot her—Sierra and her friend Jax. I hear them before I see them. The familiar laughter and loud joking haven't diminished since they disembarked at the airstrip, where I handed them over to the resort shuttle driver.

As happy as my untamable libido is to see Sierra, I'm not so thrilled to see her midriff top and extra-short shorts.

When I see some of the yachties eyeballing Sierra's ass, my attitude ratchets up from not-so-thrilled to severely annoyed. Those two drunk women are going to land themselves in some trouble.

While I watch Sierra down shots at the bar with her friend, the yachties are trying to horn in on their slightly drunken girl talk.

"Dude." Sam's been talking, and I've been rudely tuning him out. I swing back around. "Sorry, what?"

He chuckles. "I was just saying you should think about a mail order bride if you're going to stay here and work indefinitely. I know a guy."

"I don't need a mail order bride, or a dating service for that matter. Hey Sam, do me a favor. Cut those two women off," I say. "I've got a bad feeling about those two deckhands over there."

I watch as Sierra and Jax approach the bar and ask for two margaritas. Sam looks from me to them and says, "I'm sorry, ladies. I'm not allowed to keep serving once guests are visibly intoxicated. It's a safety measure. I'm so sorry."

It's a blatant lie, but it works. I watch the women slink off, only slightly disappointed. "Well, we've got donkey yoga tomorrow anyway," Jax says teasingly.

"Whatever," responds Sierra, laughing.

I watch as two yachties who've been eyeing the ladies get up and pay their tab, then follow Jax and Sierra about twenty paces behind them.

It's a long walk back to the hotel from the pier; this property is sprawling. The women stick to the lit board-walk along the beach. When we reach the hotel, I can still hear the two men mumbling and quietly laughing. Then, they rush forward to hold open the doors for them.

"Ladies," one of them says, shooting them a brilliant, white smile.

The other one says, "Let us escort you to your room."

Fortunately, the two women have enough awareness about their situation to turn them down. "Oh, that's not necessary," Jax says.

And yet, the two young men don't take a hint. I follow them upstairs and down the hallway.

Jax fumbles with her keycard, and one of the men takes it from her. "Allow me."

The other man places a hand on Sierra's back, and she freezes, eyes wide.

"That won't be necessary," I say, walking up, plucking the card away from the man, and inserting it into the card reader. "Cerulean Resort and Spa thanks you for escorting our guests back to their rooms. You can go back to your boat now."

The two white-boaters stare at me like I've just grown a third head, but then mumble, shrug, and walk away, cursing under their breath. At least they know it's better for their health to avoid lighting my fuse.

Jax shoots me a severe expression. "You're not going to try to invite yourself in for a three-way, are you? Because like we told those guys, we're not into ménage."

I am most certainly not interested in a three-way. I cast my eyes at Sierra, who smiles and bites her lip. "No. No, I'm not."

Jax sucks in a breath. "I recognize you by your voice! You're Pilot!"

Sierra blinks several times, and then recognition washes over her face. "It is you! I'm sorry, I didn't recognize you without your cap and sunglasses." She sways a bit, and I instinctively reach out to help her remain steady. When my hand brushes her hip, my pulse races.

"You're … like … really dreamy. In a bossy, take charge kind of way." Sierra's consonants are thick and slurred from the effects of the tequila.

I rub my hands together, not wanting to leave but knowing I must. No use in having a conversation she's not going to remember. "Go drink some water," I rasp, backing away and sliding my hand away from her hip.

Jax hiccups and stumbles into the room. Sierra does the world's most adorable shoulder shimmy, then says in an imitation of a breathy Marilyn Monroe, "Yes, Daddy." That pout is going to get her into trouble. But not with any random yachtie. With me.

Her lovely, if bloodshot, eyes stay locked on mine as she closes their hotel room door. I walk away frustrated as fuck, taking consolation in having done my good deed for the day.

On my way out of the hotel, I stop by the main desk to order Sierra and Jax some much-needed midnight room service: omelets, Tylenol, and the biggest bottle of water the kitchen can provide.

Chapter Four

Sierra

"WHO'S READY FOR DONKEY YOGA?!" I really shouldn't shout at the hungover Jax, who passed out on the chaise in the living area of our suite.

She smacks her lips, making that icky, dry noise that makes me cringe, but I'm ready with a glass of water and some over-the-counter meds. Opening one eye to glare at me, she takes my offerings. "Thank you."

I feel great, thanks to the hotel's surprise delivery of eggs and headache medicine last night.

After she drinks all of her water, Jax asks what time it is. I check my watch, "We have fifteen minutes to get ready for the canoe to take us to Temple Island."

Anybody else in this world as hungover as Jax would have canceled on the donkeys, but not my Jax. She gets up, downs her water, pulls her hair back, and gets ready to go. As a professional model, she's used to pulling herself together and getting the show on the road, no matter what. "Kayak. Not canoe. And I'm excited you decided to join me!"

I'm already dressed in my yoga shorts and have piled my hair up in a top knot.

Why not embrace the spirit of Jax's advice and be open to adventure? I mean, I'm not going to go looking for someone to father my baby on this island, but on the other hand, if I stay drunk for two weeks, I'll miss a hell of a lot.

"I booked a massage on the beach at Mossy Grove right after it, so as long as we're back in time, I'm good to go," I say, referring to the resort's in-house spa.

AN HOUR LATER, I'm thoroughly blissed out. Finally, I feel like I'm in vacation mode. All it took was a scenic kayak excursion, intense outdoor yoga overlooking the ocean, and giving serious scritches to some adorable donkeys on the beach at Temple Island. I was curious how donkeys would play into a yoga class; mostly, they wandered around and nuzzled everyone while we were in Downward Dog; and the yogi encouraged everyone to give pets while in Warrior pose.

The only less-than-perfect moment came when our kayak guide had to rescue Jax, who capsized her kayak at the sight of a shark that turned out to be harmless.

I bid Jax goodbye at the dock on Little Loggerhead Island as she wanders off to catch some sun on the nearest beach.

The massage turns out to be a great idea. I am lying, nearly naked, on a comfy massage table just feet away from the surf. It's wonderful. This masseuse knows her stuff, or it's been way too long since I had a massage. Probably both.

She remarks how tight my shoulders are, and we chat about what I do for a living. I tell her that I work with horses, which is partially true. I don't tell her that I volunteer at a therapy horse rescue ranch. I don't like to advertise to strangers that I don't have a proper paying job and never had. I dropped out of college and therefore failed to get the expected Mrs. degree. My parents are reluctantly "letting" me take over the family business despite my lack of a husband, but I don't much care for the family business. Real estate doesn't interest me.

"Those horses give you a workout. Your back is extremely tight."

I grunt in agreement, not because I'm rude but because I'm starting to drift off to sleep.

Just as my eyes are about to flutter closed, a tall figure looms in the entrance to the cabana.

"Howdy, Estelle. How's it hanging?"

Estelle must be the name of my masseuse because as my eyes fly open and I look over my shoulder, I see her smile, shake her head, and wave dismissively at the man.

We catch each other's eyes, and my stomach sinks. Pilot is interrupting my massage, and he's wearing a terry cloth robe just like the one the staff gave me. Well, a much bigger terry cloth robe.

"Hi?" I say.

He sees me, and his whole demeanor changes on a dime. He'd been casual and jokey with the masseuse, whom he seems to know well. The look he gives me is something close to horror, which quickly changes to stone. "Oh. I'm sorry."

I give him a perplexed look. "I'm pretty sure I booked a private massage," I say.

"I can go."

Well. He's clearly not interested in flirting with me, so no harm in letting him stay. "No, it's fine. I'm about to fall asleep anyway," I say.

A second masseur follows Pilot into the cabana, and I look the other way as he drops his towel and slides under the sheet on the second table a few feet away. This is oddly intimate, but then again, I remind myself to relax and take it in. This is island life.

Just then, my stomach drops, and my heart leaps into my throat because I suddenly remember something from last night. As I closed the door…did I call him Daddy?

I turn my face back in the direction of the other table. "I feel silly asking this, but I didn't catch your name," I say.

"Austin Fisher. And you're Sierra Kennedy."

I chuckle. "Good memory."

"I always memorize my flight manifest."

The husky way he talks sends a wave of warmth over my back, even though the breeze from the ocean wafting into our cabana feels cool at the moment.

"Nice to officially meet you, Austin Fisher."

Jax is going to get a big thank you from me later for deciding to sunbathe without me. If she were here, she'd be acting a fool trying to push this Austin Fisher and me together.

"So, how's the Babymoon so far?"

This question throws me for such a loop I nearly tumble off the massage table.

"What? How did you…?"

I trail off, not knowing what to say. But then I think, why should I be embarrassed? It's my choice to have a baby by myself, and there's nothing wrong with that.

"Guess you heard everything, huh? We thought you

couldn't hear us with that big ol' headset and the loud plane."

That's when I really take notice of Austin's face. He has kind gray eyes that crinkle when he smiles. His close-cropped hair and clean-shaven face make me think he could be ex-military. His face is tanned and weathered, just as I would imagine a bush pilot would look. He has full lips that I've yet to see break into a smile and a jaw so firm I could crack walnuts on.

"Some of the things people talk about when they think I can't hear would turn your hair white," he remarks.

My eyes widen, and I'm thrilled about the change of subject. "Like what?"

"If I told you, I'd have to kill you."

I laugh, but Austin remains serious. Then, without breaking into a smile, he says, "I'm kidding."

And now, I don't know if I'm in the presence of someone whom criminals pay to keep secrets or if he's teasing me and being awkward about it. I don't know what to make of this Austin Fisher, and that's troubling. Troubling because his energy draws me in at the same time he seems to be pulling away. That's just my dormant sensual side waking up in the presence of a rugged, stern, powerful man with a chiseled jaw. My vagina may not care that he's not interested. But I have my pride, and my vibrator.

I relax again on the table and let the masseuse's strong hands lull me back into a dreamlike state.

"By the way… thanks for getting rid of those guys. I could have handled it on my own, but things were about to get uncomfortable."

"It was nothing. Those guys were dicks, and I have to look out for guests, even when I'm on vacation."

"You're on vacation, too?"

He nods, explaining that his next chartered flight is when Jax and I go back to Pearl Island International Airport to catch our flight home.

Before I can control my mouth, I say, "You should join Jax and me on the volcano tour tomorrow," I offer.

Austin rumbles. "You don't want me hanging around like a third wheel on your girls' trip."

Adele, the masseuse, snorts. "Man wouldn't know a good opportunity if it bit him in the ass," she mutters.

Austin's masseur abruptly starts in on a chopping, deep-tissue massage that startles him. "Whoa!" he exclaims. "Careful back there."

But the male massage therapist working on Austin seems to be taking out some kind of vexation. "Adele's right. You need to loosen up. Besides, you can show the ladies around the island."

"Nobody wants me raining on their parade; not this old bush pilot," Austin says.

Why he would think that I have no idea. "I think you're being humble. I bet you're great company. Go on, tell me about your most exciting passenger. I'd love to hear it," I urge.

Austin sighs in a way that tells me he doesn't enjoy bragging about himself. "My most interesting passenger would have to be about fifty packs of diapers."

"Excuse me?"

I'm hanging on his every word, and yet I can't deny the sweet darkness that envelops me with the sound of the crashing waves. I drop out just as he's telling me about flying supplies—including diapers—into southern Florida in the aftermath of a hurricane. "No trucks or commercial jets could get in or out, so I flew with as much cargo as my little plane could carry."

I want to hear more, but soon everything is just too

cozy, and his voice is too perfect for helping me drift off to sleep. I dream about the handsome, rugged pilot transporting emergency diapers and baby formula across a ravaged seaside landscape, and I'm not going to lie. This dream is thirstier than a nap in hell.

Chapter Five

Austin

How LONG AM I going to lie here and watch Sierra sleep?

It's not as if I'm sneaking into her room like a vampire; it's not creepy, is it?

Estelle, along with my masseur, has vamoosed to let Sierra sleep for a few minutes. Estelle mentioned that Sierra had booked an extra hour just in case she fell asleep. I can't help but appreciate the way this woman thinks.

Every one of my fingers seems to itch to reach out to touch her. Sierra's freckled nose crinkles in her sleep, and that itch inside me grows into need.

I have to remind myself; she's not staying. Two weeks is just long enough to have a fling turn into full-fledged obsession. Then, what am I left with when she leaves? Fuck all.

Nobody is here to judge me, so I stare. Sierra is breathtaking when she's asleep. The rise and fall of her small bosoms. The teal polish on her toes matches the color on her fingernails. Her sun-bleached hair always falls into her face. Her eyes are closed, but I can tell you what color they are: the same turquoise as the ocean out there.

A stiff breeze wafts over her body, and I notice the goose flesh that spreads over her arm that rests outside of the sheet. In her sleeping state, Sierra rolls to her side and hunkers down. When she does, the sheet falls open and exposes one small, tan nipple. Oh. Shit.

I slide off my table and throw on my robe. Careful not to wake Sierra, I tug the fabric gently back over her chest. I freeze as she mumbles something in her sleep and adjusts. If she wakes up, I'm screwed. I'm officially a creep.

The sheet falls again. Because of gravity. Dummy.

I shouldn't look. But, I shouldn't do a lot of things. And I can't help but notice that nipple is erect. I'm not such a self-centered son of a bitch to think that pretty little nub is looking for me. The breeze is to blame more than anything. But the sight of it sends a jolt of electricity into my chest that shoots down into my midsection and lands squarely in my dick. That's all I need, for her to wake up and see me pitching a tent. Or worse, see this log peeking out of my robe, like a perv.

Up close, I catch the coconut-lime scent of the massage oil all over her, and my mouth waters at the thought of tasting her. There's only one thing to do. I raise the sheet to her chin, and then she does something so sweet it grips every muscle in my chest. Sierra scrunches up her body into a fetal position and hugs the sheet close, making a faint sighing noise.

I tighten the belt of my robe and check to make sure all limbs are safely hidden as I make my way to the entrance of the cabana. As I turn my back, she mutters something, clearly in her sleep: a small giggle followed by, "Hmm, Pilot Daddy Austin."

Just then, her friend Jax breezes in.

"Whoa! Well, hello! Couples massage?" Jax's smile is expectant.

I shake my head. "Just a coincidence. How was donkey yoga?"

She seems surprised and pleased. "You and Sierra have been talking, I see. It was great, thanks for asking."

I move to step out, eager to disappear.

"Austin?"

Sierra, now awake and sitting up on the massage table, grips her sheet to her body. Her hair is over one eye, and the tanned skin of her chest glistens with massage oil. With mussed hair, the sheet barely covering her breasts as she perches on the massage table, Sierra resembles my memory of how she appeared after sex last night—in my dream.

Her saying my name like that feels like she's carving hers into the rough layer of bark that protects my heart.

Taking my leave of the two friends, I nod to Jax and shoot a wink at Sierra. "Have fun at the volcano, you two. But be careful; The island god loves virgins."

Sierra looks at me wide-eyed, and then both she and Jax cackle as I walk away.

Chapter Six

Sierra

I THOUGHT Austin was kidding about the virgin thing.

It turns out, even Brooks, the tour guide, mentions it.

"Before this area was known as The Pearl Crescent islands, a legend was born when seafaring scavengers discovered Little Loggerhead Island in 1769. A particularly ruthless Dutch sea captain was closing in on the pirates to reclaim some gold they had stolen. So the pirates buried their treasure on the south end of the island. Just as they buried it, the earth beneath grew so hot it blistered their feet. The ship's captain stayed on the island, but the rest of the crew retreated to Severed Key on the far edge of the fringe and waited out the eruption. When several strange occurrences led them to believe some deity had cursed them, they returned to find the entire area where the treasure had been buried under molten rock. Meanwhile, their ship suffered storm damage, the crew suffered starvation, and a giant squid attacked the boat.

"So a year later, the band of pirates returned to the volcano and tossed their youngest sailor into the abyss. Legend says that a fissure formed in the volcanic rock right before their eyes, which they followed to their clearing and allowed them to recover their pirate captain's body. They never found the treasure, but the curse was lifted. The island god allowed the pirates to stay."

Jax whispers in my ear, "That is totally made up."

"If it's not, it's seriously *fucked* up," I whisper back.

A nearby woman in the tour group turns and shoots Jax and me a dirty look for whispering curse words.

Jax sees the look and mutters, "She should pay more attention to her kid instead of worrying about a few curse words."

I turn to look, and I see that child playing right by the edge of the trail, overlooking a steep descent into the crater.

I hang back a little as the group slowly shuffles along a dirt path that circles the rim of the volcano. Ahead, the trail narrows, hugging the inside of the mouth, spiraling in circles around the massive crater. The dormant volcano teems with life: Birds, reptiles, flowering trees of all kinds that I've never seen before. It's going to be a pleasant, shady, if slightly humid, trek down to the bottom, where we're scheduled to swim in a hot spring and eat a picnic lunch. From there, we're supposed to follow an underground tunnel to the outside, where golf carts will be available to drive back to the hotel.

To both my and Jax's surprise, Austin is here, but of course, still behaving like his aloof and stoic self. Why did he even bother to show up if he's so blasé about it? A strange knot forms in my stomach; it's because he felt obligated to join us after our massage therapists teased him about my invitation. And now, it feels like I've been chasing him, which I have not.

Impossibly, Austin seems even more distant than usual, but then again, his aviators hide a lot.

Finally, I see what's got him preoccupied. He's watching the errant kid.

The kid, whose name is Isaac from what I've gathered from his older sister's scolding of him, is ignoring his sister's admonishments. "Isaac! You're missing it. The part about the island gods."

Isaac is far more interested in examining a giant tortoise that has ambled up the path. He mounts it like it's a horse, and the tour guide stops talking.

"In 1877—Please get off the tortoise before you injure him. Now, where was I?" Unlike a lot of the overly accommodating resort employees, I can tell Brooks pulls no punches when guests are misbehaving.

The mom scoffs, "Well, you don't have to be so sharp with him. He's only seven."

Surprising me, Jax claps back in defense of our tour guide. "Well, if you won't supervise your kid, someone has to."

I glance over at the mom, who looks like she's about to take off her earrings. Jax looks back at her as if she's daring her to make a move. Austin is smirking, apparently looking forward to a catfight.

That's when it happens.

Isaac, the little shit, slides off the tortoise's back and, with a loud "Whee!" goes tumbling down the wall of the crater.

"Isaac!" the dad shouts while the mom screams.

Then everyone in the group is panicking and rushing to the edge.

When I look down, little Isaac has slid down the

earthen slope on his stomach, slowed by the friction of soil and rocks and small plants. He is unhurt and indeed looks as if he's having the time of his life.

I watch as Austin curses, then climbs down after him. "Hang on," he mutters as if this happens every day.

We all watch as Austin grabs hold of a vining plant and lowers himself down, calmly talking to Isaac the entire time. Isaac's feet slip around on a mossy rock, but he's holding on to the base of a small tree.

Austin is about three feet above the kid. "Isaac, buddy, how are you doing?"

The kid responds, and for the first time, sounds a little worried. "I'm…I'm okay."

Austin is trying to hang on while holding onto the line and unwind it. He finally has enough slack let out that he can drop it down to Isaac. I'm sweating so much my whole body is soaked. Even though this is a tense moment, I can't keep my eyes from traveling down to those mountain climber calves.

Not the time, Sierra, I think to myself.

The vine drops down to where Isaac is, but just as he's about to grab for the vine, his feet slip in the mud three more feet. The entire group shrieks in fright. Austin gives up on the vine idea and then inches his way down. He's just going to grab this kid, somehow.

Thank god Isaac is now staying put. I look over at his mom, and I can't help it; I feel a little sad for her. Sure, she should've been watching her kid, but no mother deserves to go through this. Finally, Austin has climbed down to where Isaac is, and carefully he loads the kid on his back.

"Okay, buddy?"

The kid's voice is shaky, but he says he's okay.

With the kid on his back, Austin begins his slow, careful climb up the cliff. The tour guide has climbed down to meet them halfway, having lashed himself to a tree near the top of the cliff. He reaches down and grasps Austin's hand, and the two big, masculine arms strain as they together work to pull themselves and the child to safety. When all three reach the trail at the cliffside, the tour guide passes the kid off to Isaac's father as Austin slumps over in a heap.

Everyone else rushes around Isaac and his family, making sure he's okay. The tour guide is checking him over for injuries.

Me? I'm checking on Austin.

Chapter Seven

Austin

If I take Sierra's offered hand, I'm just going to drag her down here with me. She's a welcome sight after what just happened. I have the urge to tug her down here on the ground with me and kiss her until I stop trembling in abject terror.

But studying her face, she's just concerned for me, an old man who just did a thing he never thought he was capable of.

She's probably feeling sorry for me as I wince and wave off her help. I come to standing and try not to make it evident that my entire body hurts. Dammit. Forty is not the new twenty, that's for sure.

"That was incredible," she says. Her lovely eyes are wide as they gaze up at me.

"Anybody here would have done the same thing."

She shakes her head. "You were quicker on your feet and…very agile. You saved his life."

Not going to lie; that does puff up my ego a bit.

"Well, thanks for saying that, I guess," I say.

She laughs. "No. Thank you for doing what you did. He would have died."

I shrug. "He probably wouldn't have died. Most likely would have just slid all the way to the bottom and then fell into the hot spring. Provided he can swim, he would have lived."

She covers her mouth, but her eyes are laughing. I can't believe we're having this conversation three feet away from Isaac and his family.

The Isaac family heads back up to the mountain top, where they will be cutting off their adventures for the day with a ride back to the hotel. Brooks looks pale and shaken.

"Austin, do you mind escorting these ladies the rest of the way down to the spring while I take the family back up to the rim?"

Sierra looks up at me and sees me hesitating. "Try not to squirm. I'm not the worst body to ever wear a swimsuit."

The truth is I'd rather have my teeth pulled than be forced to see her in a bikini.

Not because she wouldn't look good. But because she's fucking gorgeous. And sweet. And too damn tempting.

But, it's evident to everyone that Brooks needs help, and I'm nothing if not a helper.

"Yeah. Yeah, sure, buddy. No problem." My voice is strangely dry and more raspy than usual. Grudgingly, I decide it'll all be okay if her friend is with her. No funny business in the hot spring, then. I can be a disinterested lifeguard; that's it. I'm a grown-ass man in charge of my urges and desires, after all.

Brooks radios for the golf cart to meet him and Isaac's family at the mountain top. "All right. I'll take them back to the hotel. You just radio me when you're done with your swim."

"I'll join you," Jax says to Brooks. My stomach falls into my feet.

Sierra calls after her friend, "Wait, where are you going? I wanna finish the tour!"

Jax turns around and says, "You and your new friend can finish the tour together. One on one." She then curtsies and slips her arm through the tour guide's arm, chattering away as they trek back up the trail.

Sierra's mouth gapes as she watches them go, then turns to me.

"We can skip the swim if you want," I say.

She arches an eyebrow. "Listen, I didn't spend half the day in a humid crater, only to pass up the chance to swim in a volcanic hot spring. I am already in my swimsuit under these shorts. Besides, you're my tour guide, now. You have to be there to protect me from the island gods."

Fuck. It's not the island gods she should be worried about.

THE BOTTOM of the trail spills out into a wide landing at the edge of the cloudy blue pool. I've visited this spot many times before, but I've never seen the caverns through someone else's eyes.

"This might be the most beautiful place I've ever seen in my entire life," Sierra says.

I walk around the edge of the pool and look for a spot to lay out the blanket to sit on for our lunch. Hopefully, she won't want to swim first. Maybe I can convince her to eat and then wait for twenty minutes because of the whole stomach cramp thing. I know it's a myth, but perhaps I can stall for as long as possible.

Looking back, I see Sierra pulling off her top and dropping her shorts, revealing the same style of string bikini I saw on her that day we first met. Only, it's a bright purple color, and she makes it look magnificent next to her hair and skin.

All the important bits are covered, but only just. The thin layer of purple could disappear with a single tug of that string.

And everything about Sierra conspires to tug away at the layers that have protected me from giving in to temptation.

I'm not a religious man, but I'm praying to the island gods for help now.

Even worse than silence, I picture their response to be nothing but knowing laughter.

Fuckers.

Chapter Eight

Sierra

"Come on in; the water's fine."

The whole place is so perfect I might never leave. The rock sediment gives the water a magical, bluish-white look —the walls of the cavern sparkle with it. I feel as if I'm in some secret hidden dragon's lair.

Austin's having trouble looking at me. "I didn't bring my trunks. I've been down here so many times; I'm sort of over it."

I splash him playfully from where I tread water. "Jaded much?"

"I'm probably not as charming as the kind of guys you're used to. Sorry about that," he says.

His eyes dart everywhere except to me, and I have to work hard not to grab him and pull him into the water.

"You could just skinny dip if you want. I won't tell anyone."

I could be mistaken, but I think I see his lip twitch, and a flush of pink crawl across his neck. I wish he would look at me with those clear blue eyes. I also kind of want to rub that short-short crop of hair on his head. He's all lean muscle, and despite him mocking himself for his aging body, there's not an ounce of fat on him or any sign that he's less a man than he used to be. Not that I knew the man before. I wish I had. I like talking to him.

And I did promise Jax I would get good and reckless.

I smile up at Austin mischievously and I dive underwater, swimming across to the other side and back again.

"It's okay if you don't like my company. I don't mind swimming alone," I say. Okay, I admit; I'm laying it on pretty thick.

But it works.

Austin makes a strange noise from somewhere deep in his chest. "All right, turn around."

I'm thrilled and surprised, so of course, I do as he says. I swivel and face the far wall and listen.

"No peeking," he orders.

"I would never," I say, chuckling. Though in my mind, I've got a complete picture of those shorts sliding down his legs, and I feel a twinge of need between mine.

I don't turn to look until I hear the splash.

"Told you it was nice!"

If I thought he looked sexy and outdoorsy before, Austin soaking wet only enhances all of that by a thousand.

I watch as he glides through the water, cutting through it smoothly like a sea lion. "Are you part merman?" I laugh. "You look like freaking Aquaman in the water. I look like Ursula."

He thinks for a second. "Ursula's cool, though. She's got her own thing going on."

I splash him playfully. "Wrong answer," I shout, though I'm not offended. I know what he means. "But that's about how I feel next to Jax in a bikini."

Austin looks confused. "What do you mean?"

"Legs for days. Not to mention the boobs. It might make me feel better if I could remind myself that her boobs are fake, but they're not."

Despite the already hot water, the temperature seems to rise the more I speak because the smoldering from Austin's eyes is about ten degrees hotter than anything in this cavern.

"Can I say something you're not going to like?"

I suck in a breath. "I don't know if I'm ready for this. Lay it on me."

The look on his face is one of pure unadulterated sincerity. Where's the stoic pilot who strolled into the middle of my massage session? Did he change, or am I getting to know him better? Or is he showing more of himself to me?

"I think you're brave deciding to have a baby on your own."

I cringe. "You're right. I don't like that word. There's nothing brave about me. I've got the money and the time. I don't have a real job, so it's not like I'll need child care."

Austin stares at me. "So? Who gives a shit. You're making a huge decision by yourself, and that's brave whether you like to hear it or not."

I sigh. "Brave or crazy?"

The grunt from him feels like a warning that he wants me to stop putting myself down. "You need to feel both scared and crazy to have a kid either way. And the world needs more people like you to have kids—people who are aware of how huge that decision is. And, people who are nice and kind and can pass on more goodness into the world."

I have to inhale deeply because my brain needs more oxygen to absorb what he just said. Did he get hit on the head by a coconut when he was rescuing that kid earlier? "That might be the nicest thing anyone has ever said to me—"

"Well, I didn't say it to be nice—"

"—and if you don't kiss me this instant—"

I don't have to elaborate any further.

And just like that, no more talking. The only sounds in this cavern are from our breathing and from the curious explorations of Austin's lips on mine.

Every inch of my skin seems to hum. My brain turns to mush, and I forget what we were talking about.

It's not easy to keep kissing when my feet don't touch the bottom.

As if reading my mind, he pulls away from the kiss and says, "Follow me."

We swim to the other side, where there's a small rocky ledge beneath the surface of the water. I swim over to it and hoist myself up to sit next to him. Now I'm a little chilly because I'm exposed to the cool cave air.

I let out a little involuntary shiver, and Austin sees it. His arms circle around me, closing me in, hemming me in from the lower temperatures. He further warms me with movement of his mouth against mine. Austin kisses my top lip, then my bottom, then both cheeks, which makes me grin stupidly. The next time he kisses my bottom lip, his tongue slides against it, and his teeth nip me there, just a touch.

The wicked dipping of his tongue stokes the fire between my thighs. I let out a sigh and another shiver.

Austin takes this as a sign that I'm still cold and flattens me against his chest, letting go of the kiss to wrap me up in a warm hug. "You cold?"

"No." My lashes flutter against his chest where he grips me, and I hear the strange growling noise again coming from his chest.

"You're lying," he says. When his lips find mine again, he feels as if his body demands it. With my eyes closed, I feel his hands grip my face. My arms circle his torso; I don't dare hug him any lower because he's naked and I don't want to brush up against anything I shouldn't. Actually, yes, I do want to do that, but I'm not going to. Not yet anyway.

I'm astounded that he can kiss me so passionately and not try to grope me anywhere else. I would like him to grope me, pet me, do all sorts of things. But he's such a gentleman; I'm afraid to take the lead away from him.

The next time his tongue touches my lip, I open my mouth and slip the tip of my tongue out to do the same to him. A slight groan escapes his throat, and our tongues tangle in a warm, sensual dance. Sparks of pleasure glide all over from the roots of my hair down to my toes, spiking my nipples into tight little nubs. I'm letting loose, and I'm happy.

We pull away from the kiss, breathless.

Austin's mouth shines with my sheer lip gloss.

I dab away some of the gloss with my thumb, and my filthy mind conjures an image. No, don't go there, horny brain. Don't you start wondering if this is how he might look after going downtown. If his sheer commitment to kissing is any indication, then the other stuff. Oh lord…

"What are you looking at me like that for?" he says.

Just then, my stomach rolls and gurgles, and the sound is made worse by the echoing inside this cavernous space.

"You're hungry," he says. "Lunchtime."

I am hungry. But not for food. I'm hungry for this man to put his hands on me and drop the gentlemanly act. I want him to be ruthless with me. Pull me on top of him and make me scream. Cause a cave-in. Bring this volcano back to life. Hold me down against the floor and look for buried treasure in my pussy.

God, what's wrong with you, Sierra?

I nod dumbly.

He kisses me one more time. I'm so hot all over that I hope it's just a peck—the kiss of a dead fish. But of course, it's not. It's a deep, full, thorough, arousing tongue kiss. Oh god. It's so good. And leaves me wanting so much more. I heard the groan from him; I know this is not enough. So why is he swimming away from me now? Who cares about lunch?

Maybe I'm not a good enough kisser for him. Perhaps he was testing the waters, and he's not that into me.

I watch him swim to the other side of the underground spring, and I wait for him to hop out of the water first. Brazenly, I watch him. Austin's round, mountain-climber's backside and muscular thighs sear into my brain. He's taking his time like he knows I'm watching.

"You can use my towel," I tell him. The idea of sharing a towel with a random man would gross me out under normal circumstances. It doesn't seem to bother me now, not after swapping spit. I hop down from the ledge until I'm submerged once again from the neck down, and I tread water, rubbing my thighs together like a horny teenager. His back is still to me, shaking water off his legs. Watching this, I fight the urge to reach my hand down between my legs. Until I stop fighting. I just go ahead and do it. My hand slides down inside my bikini bottom, and with my eyes trained on him, I do the deed while watching him dress. The way he's bent over, sliding his shorts back on, I'm in no doubt this floor show is for my benefit.

Seconds later, the pleasure washes over me as I bite down on my bottom lip so hard I'm afraid I might bleed.

Chapter Nine

Austin

THE COFFEE at Mello Toast is the best on any of the islands of The Pearl Crescent. The corporate coffee in the city on Pearl Island can keep their burnt beans. The resort has its good restaurants, but this is where the locals go for brunch.

I sit outside and stare at the waves, thinking about what I did wrong with Sierra yesterday. I shouldn't have kissed her like that. My feelings got the better of me; I can't be alone with her like that anymore. It's wise if we only see each other in public because I can't be trusted.

It serves me right that she was unusually reserved and quiet all through lunch and for the entire drive back to the hotel.

She was so quiet that I had started to feel guilty for kissing her the way I did. So remorseful that I apologized for being so forward with her. She'd simply pursed her lips, studying me for a moment, and then went up to her room.

I sip my coffee and gaze out onto the waves, considering whether I should try again and be more clear about why I was apologetic.

And then, who should walk into the Mello Toast but her. Sierra.

I set down my coffee, sit back in my chair, and take in the welcome sight of her. She has a strange, avid look in her eye. Her black, embroidered cover-up flaps in the sea breeze, and her hair is twisted into a bun on top of her head. Her face is flushed like she's already been walking the beach and had too much sun this morning.

Sierra looks like she wants to tell me something about as much as I want to tell her something.

I stand up and offer her a seat across from me.

"Hi," she says. "I think I ought to apologize."

"I think you need to rethink that," I reply, prompting her brow to furrow in confusion.

When the server brings her a coffee, she nods sweetly up at her, then grips the mug in both hands and sniffs. Her nostrils flare like a rabbit before she takes an appreciative sip. Every freckle, every twitch, makes me fall deeper and deeper. I want to make coffee for her every morning just to watch her do that thing with her face. I want to sit across our shared kitchen table and just marvel at her.

"Austin, it's okay if you're not into me. I shouldn't have made you feel obligated to kiss me yesterday."

I down the rest of my coffee and rub my tummy. It was rumbling for some fresh scrambled eggs a minute ago, but right now, I can't eat a bite until I say what I have to say to Sierra.

"Sweetheart, listen. You might think that the kissing was your idea. But trust me, I'd been thinking about kissing you since the second I saw you."

Sierra's eyes flash, and she looks down into the depths

of her black coffee. She chuckles, "Guess I'm not all that bad to look at in a swimsuit after all."

She's not getting it. So I'm going to be straight with her, throwing all caution to the wind. I'm still not interested in being her vacation fling. I don't know what this is between us, but it's real, no matter how I try to avoid it. "No," I say. "I meant the second I met you on the tarmac. That's when I knew I liked you. That's the first time I wanted to kiss you. You asking didn't matter; it was going to happen. What does matter now is what do we do about this?"

With wide, scared, and curious eyes, she rasps, "Do about what?"

"About the fact that I can't stop thinking about you. About the fact that I try to avoid you, to be professional, not letting myself get tangled up in a fling with you because you're leaving the island in a week and a half."

A mischievous smile spreads across her face. "That all sounds like a personal problem for you to figure out because it's causing you to send mixed signals."

"How so?"

"Well," Sierra explains, fidgeting with the handle of her coffee mug. "I thought you weren't into me. You kissed me yesterday, and then you stopped. So I thought we would be friends, and I was trying to be okay with that. So …You mean you liked the kiss?"

I'm about ready to knock over the table and grab her by the shoulders. "Sierra, are you for real? I…just…I mean… God, I've never been this tongue-tied around anyone. You mess with my head, and I don't know what to say, and when I do talk, I say the wrong things. Fuck. I'm waking up in the middle of the night, after having dreams that I'm asking you to—" I cut myself off, but her eyes beckon me to continue.

"Asking me to what, Austin?"

It's too soon to admit this … but fuck it. It's the island magic, making me blurt it out. "To let me be the one to put a baby in you."

Sierra stares back at me, blinking.

People at a nearby table turn and smirk. Another table titters. Someone gasps and drops a fork, and still others laugh.

She folds her hands flat on the table and looks down at her fingers.

I scrape my hands over my scalp. "Well, that could've been phrased better."

Chapter Ten

Sierra

I SPENT the last 12 hours thinking he wasn't into me, but he is?

I whisper though it's futile because everyone around us at Mello Toast is listening. "Are these just wild, wet dreams, or is there more to it than that?"

Austin shakes his head, blows out a breath, and darts his eyes to the blue sky above as if seeking answers.

"Yes."

"That's not an answer," I say.

"It means yes to both. I can't believe I'm saying it, but you broke me, Sierra. Every time I close my eyes, I'm making you pregnant. I'm sorry. I can't keep my distance when we're together. You put inappropriate thoughts into my head. So we've either got to get this out of our system, or we've got to explore this thing between us."

"I gotta go," I say, standing and backing away.

"For how long?" Austin's Adam's apple bobs up and

down. I hate that I'm making him feel anxious, but what
does he expect?

I look at him over my shoulder as I walk away. "A
woman takes as long as she needs. I'll need to make a
pro/con list."

IT'S TRUE. I do need to make a pro/con list. Because what
Austin has said to me is preposterous.

Having fun is one thing. A lifelong commitment around
a shared child is another.

But then again: did he actually ask me, or was he
simply telling me about his dreams? His only clear suggestion was to "explore this thing between us."

I tap my marker against my lip because it helps me
think. Does his suggestion fit the mission of Babymoon
or not?

"That legal pad is going to get soaked."

I look up at Jax, who is standing on the platform at the
stern of the speedboat, being fitted into her wet suit.

"Pro: he's smart. Con: he's a little too humble."

Jax snorts as she zips herself in. "As if humble is a bad
thing. If anything, we need more humans with a little bit
of humility."

I love that she doesn't see the irony in her words,
considering she has such an intensely hot body that she
looks gorgeous even in a wet suit. "I disagree. We need
more people who know their worth. Like you."

She rolls her eyes. "All right, moving along. We don't
need to get into one of your philosophical discussions;
we're about to go parasailing for the first time. Now put
that away and soak it up."

I perk up. "Philosophical discussions…That's it! He's

not a big talker but when he does talk? He's intense. Also, a good listener."

Jax cocks her head at me. "Are you making a pro/con list for his sperm or a relationship?"

"Do you have to be so crass?"

"Sierra, have you met me?"

"Have I met the version of Jax who is about to go parasailing even though she's terrified of heights? No. Never met her."

"Haha. Have fun with your list. And while you're at it, you need to change that list heading from 'Having sex with Austin' to 'Having a relationship with Austin.' Because that's where you're headed, and for the record, I approve all of the above."

I stare at my friend. This is illogical. Austin might say he wants to explore this chemistry between us, but he makes no sense.

"Con: he's delusional."

Jax shakes her head at me, then blows me a kiss, and she's in the water.

"Pro list: he's direct and says exactly what he wants." I say this out loud even though I'm alone with Brooks, who steers this vessel. I remind myself I'm in paradise, and there are zero repercussions for what I'm talking about out loud.

"Con: I don't know what I want.

"Pro: adventurous spirit.

"Con: I barely know him."

I tap my marker against my lip and stare behind the boat. There, I see something I never thought I would see: Jax, sailing over the water, the wind in her hair, forgetting that she is afraid of heights and having the time of her life.

Next, it's my turn.

Chapter Eleven

Sierra

"MAY I?"

I look up from where I'm lounging at the beach, and it's a vaguely familiar-looking man towering over me. My heart leaps for a second, thinking that it's Austin. My pulse calms down when I see it's not him. My eyes flick down to his wrist, where he wearsthe official wristband for the resort. He's gesturing to the empty lounger next to me.

I tell him he can join me as long as he doesn't mind giving up the chair when my friend arrives in a few minutes.

"That's okay; this will only take a few minutes," he says.

I laugh. "Why does this sound strangely menacing?"

The man squats down to face me, and I recognize him then as a memory from our first night on the pier comes back. "Wait a minute, I know you," I say. "You were at the bar the other night." Not one of the kids from the yacht, but some other guys we also talked to briefly.

He looks a little too proud of himself and tugs at the buttons of his polo. "I'm flattered you remember me."

Absentmindedly, I say, "We talked to so many people."

We share an uncomfortable silence, in which he looks like he's waiting for me to engage him in some sort of conversation. I wait it out. I'm not about to fill the silence with patter. Not my style.

"Burke Belcher," he says, holding out his hand. "I was hoping you'd actually remember me from earlier. Like, way earlier. in fact."

"Really?"

"You're Sierra Kennedy. Surely, you remember my family?"

This is where I should get up and run away, but I'm curious how the hell this guy knows me. "Where did you get that impression? Should I?"

He laughs and nods, and I get an intensely creepy feeling that he's about to admit he's a Class A stalker. "My family is in the real estate business. Our families go way back; we've worked on several projects together."

The hairs on my neck stand up. "Excuse me, how do you know who I am?"

He shrugs goodnaturedly, but I'm completely spooked. "Your father might have mentioned your little vacation to my father. My partner and I recently sold our tech company, so we're celebrating by traveling around the world, so we thought we'd make a pit stop and say hello. You probably heard of our startup; my family brags about it endlessly."

He tells me the company's name, but I have no clue what he's talking about. He launches into a long description, none of it I understand. He speaks for about five minutes and doesn't stop to ask me a single thing about me or what I'm doing here.

"I'm really not involved in my family's business, so I'm sorry if I have no clue what you're talking about at all."

Burke, in his way, also has not a clue. "No worries. Just thought I'd do your dad a favor and put myself out there as another option for your … family planning."

Oh. My. God. My parents somehow coerced a work colleague's son travel all this way as a last ditch effort to keep me from having a baby out of wedlock. As much as all of this throws me for a loop, I shouldn't be surprised. My father is a world class manipulator. And fearful. More than anything, he fears anything that might reflect poorly on the family.

I have to ask. "And you're just okay with being asked to present yourself to me like a prize race horse?"

This guy is completely bewildering. "Well, I am the third most eligible billionaire under 40 in the Financial Times."

I squint at him. "The Financial Times has a list of eligible bachelors?" This day gets weirder by the second.

Thank god, here comes Jax, soaked through to the skin and looking invigorated after …whatever she and Brooks got up to after we went parasailing.

"Hey!" I wave at her like I'm half-mad, just to be sure to get her attention.

She spots me and comes running up. I wish Brooks were with her, but alas, he is not.

Burke turns and sees Jax. "Here comes trouble," he says.

What does that even mean when people say that? He doesn't even know us.

He turns to me and says, "It's been wonderful talking to you, and I wondered if I could buy you a drink tonight."

"You're in my seat," Jax says, her voice slightly edged with impatience.

With that, Burke stands and nods to both of us. "Well, hope to see you two tonight at Calypso. Should be worth your while."

"Holy shit, you look hot!" The compliment comes from Jax, I glance down at my new bikini, and I admit it is the most risqué item of clothing I may have ever owned. All that's separating my tits from direct ultraviolet rays is a piece of white cloth about the width of a man's palm. The triangle of fabric on the bottom is even smaller. A shiver runs down my spine when I think too hard about that comparison.

"Thanks," I say to my friend, who is graciously blocking the sun from my eyes as I look her up and down. "And you look hot too. Like a very hot, very wet drowned kitten."

"Kitten!"

"I thought 'drowned rat' was insulting."

"I'll take it," Jax says, plopping down on the lounge chair that I'm saving for her. I've packed a small cooler of water and snacks, and she immediately digs it. "Wow, thanks, mama," she says through a mouthful of cheese and tomato sandwich that I assembled from the small grocery store at the resort.

"You're welcome."

"So, Brooks has a nature lesson with the kids at DragonZone after lunch, but after that, he's free. Are you still up for a foraging tour?"

I smile though my eyes are closed as I'm enjoying the heat and the rays. "You're spending every waking moment with that man if at all possible. Are you sure it's just a fling? Are you sure you're not filling every possible moment, so you don't have to think about the fallout of skipping your wedding?"

Jax lifts one shoulder but can't fool me as I turn my head to check her expression. The smile creeping across her face is a dead giveaway.

"You like him," I say.

"Yeah. I thought this was just going to be a casual vacation thing. I even told Brooks about my rather bizarre circumstances—well, some of it—and he's unfazed."

She seems happy, which is something I haven't seen from her in a while. She might be a successful model in her own right, but her life back in the States is out of control. Through no fault of her own, she's been caught up in the shady dealings of her music producer father. It's truly appalling the expectations they put on her. I have a feeling Jax is going to extend her time on the island.

"He's not your usual type," I say, thinking of the slightly nerdy Brooks and his tendency to talk endlessly about birds, flowers, tree frogs.

All of a sudden, another presence is blocking out the sun. I look up, and the familiar shape of Austin Fisher is silhouetted against the azure South Pacific sky. "Hi," I say.

"We need to talk," he says.

"Yes, we do," I say.

"Are you finished with your pro/con list?"

"Yes."

If I thought this day couldn't get any weirder, I'm now being kidnapped.

Austin has thrown a beach blanket over me and is lifting me into the air without another word.

"What are you doing?"

He doesn't say. He simply scares the liver out of me by tossing me over his shoulder and carrying me away from the beach, wrapped up in a blanket like a burrito.

"You've had enough sun."

"Where are you taking me?!"

"Out of the sun."

"Can you put me down, please? And be more specific?"

Austin sets me down when we've reached a stand of shady trees set back from the beach.

I huff in disgust and unwrap myself, shoving the blanket at him. "Was that necessary?" I bluster. "I can talk to you just fine from my lounge chair at the beach."

"Not in that outfit, you can't."

"It's an adults-only section of the beach. I'm not corrupting anyone by being there with a two-piece."

"My god, it's not a two-piece. It's barely one-piece."

"Thank you, I wasn't sure if I could pull it off, but now that it's getting terrible reviews from you, I'll go take it off and wear my caftan for the rest of the trip."

He grits his teeth and tells me, "You don't know what you're doing. You don't get the assholes who come here. They're all staring at you. It's disrespectful."

"Well, that's their problem, not mine. And I do know what I'm doing. You don't even know what was happening back there. That guy was sent here by my father to talk me out of artificial insemination. Trust me, I didn't do anything to get his attention, and he's not going to be bothering us anymore."

This news throws him. "He was? Do you want me to get rid of him?"

Still mad as a wet hen, I bluster, "I can take care of myself!"

Austin points aggressively at the beach. "Guys like that are not going to do anything unholy toward you out in the open on the beach. They're going to wait until they get you alone, at night or in a private spot, weasel their way into your room, and then they take advantage of you. Over-power you."

"You're reaching," I say.

Austin scrapes the tips of his fingers of both hands through his hair and blurts out an odd, guttural-sounding growl.

"You're not getting it."

"This place is crawling with security. I'm pretty certain there are cameras everywhere."

"That's not my primary concern."

I flail my arms in exasperation. "Then what is your major concern, Captain Fisher?"

"That I can't stand it when you're clueless, and another jerkoff is flirting with you."

My eyes flash at Austin's face, which looks ferocious. "You're jealous."

"Damn right," he growls.

We stare at each other for half a minute, neither of us saying anything. Enormous flower bushes surround the little copse of trees; the sand feels cool under my feet.

I turn and look, but I can't see the beach from here. The boardwalk is about thirty feet away.

A cool ocean breeze rushes through, sending a palm leaf brushing against my body. My nipples react at the unexpected light touch. Austin's gaze falls, and he sees it. My nipples are probably high beams at the moment. How pathetic that I'm so hard up that foliage arouses me.

"I'm going back out there for a swim," I say, unable to hide my smirk. I just want to see what Austin might do. The untamed look in his eye is turning me on, and I want to see how far I can push.

He grips me under my upper arm. "Not in that, you're not."

"Stop me, then. I dare you." I can feel my lips

pulsating with blood, and my hands itch to touch that chest in front of me.

The next thing I know, I'm backed up against a palm tree, Austin's hands in my hair and his mouth pressed against mine in a searing kiss. If I wondered how jealous he was, now I know. He's so jealous he's angry. Oh, he's not hurting me, but he's kissing me so hard that my nearly bare back feels every bump on the trunk of this tree, and his chest is flat against mine. Guess I got my wish. I run my hands up Austin's sides, stroking his back and coming around to the sides of his chest. He kisses like a man on fire, his tongue darting into my mouth insistently.

He pulls back and still has that wild look in his eye. Austin keeps his hands locked in my hair and drags wet, sultry kisses down my neck. I feel overcome by his sheer urgency. If I had any doubt I was an object of his desire, those doubts are banished.

He tastes like the salty sea, and he crashes into me so thoroughly I want to drown in his touch, his taste, his hunger, his demanding mouth.

"Sierra." Just hearing him say my name sends sparks rushing everywhere through my body.

"Captain."

He smiles down at me wickedly, grinding his pelvis against me. "I like it when you call me that."

"Captain, are you gonna let me go back to the beach?"

"Not until I split you open so good that there won't be a man or woman on this island that won't smell me all over you and know you're fuckin' mine. Mine. Now, let's go to your room."

I bite my lip, thinking.

"What's on your mind, sweet Sierra?"

"I said I wanted to get crazy on my Babymoon."

When I say the word "baby," I feel the long, thick rod jerk against my pelvis.

He rumbles, "Here? Outside?"

"No one can see us."

"They can hear us."

"Well, Captain, you're just going to have to control yourself when I make you shout my name."

He looks down at me, eyes hooded, as a low growl vibrates in his chest. "Fuck me," he says.

In response, I slide my leg up the outside of his thigh. Captain Fisher has my legs wrapped around his hips and claims my mouth once again without another word.

Both breathless, he pulls back far enough to reach between us and tug my bikini bottoms to the side. "Fuck, this is no more than a string." He strums it like a guitar string, and the touch of his rough fingers against my sensitive skin sends a rush of slickness all over my folds.

I pout. "Don't you like it?"

Austin Fisher is a filthy, dirty, jealous man, and I wouldn't want him any other way. He holds my gaze as his hands explore, fingers probing, his thumb circling my clit. I gasp every time he hits that tight, aching spot that's only grown needier with our grappling. I don't look down but stay focused on his eyes; I hear him unzip. And then sigh as he pulls out his cock. I lick my lips; his part with arousal. His arm moves and flexes, and I know what he's doing. I'm insanely jealous of that stroking hand.

"How dare you be jealous of men chatting with me when that greedy hand is gripping you instead of me."

With a grunt of effort, I find myself fully seated on his cock without another warning. I'm filled, shocked, and aroused beyond reason. I barely register the scrape of the tree bark against my back There's no one and nothing but us. Austin and me. Urgent. Fast. Rough, but also sweet.

One thrust up reminds me I'm against a tree. I try not to wince at the scratchiness, but Austin sees it and immediately goes into caretaker mode. "Baby, are you okay?"

Breathless, I tell him I'm fine. But he doesn't believe me, and now we're switched. He's up against the tree, and I'm riding him still. How is this possible? How does this man have the kind of upper body strength…

Oh, but another thrust into me, and I forget all my logical questions. I don't know how Austin's going to thrust while I am balancing on him like a howler monkey, but somehow he manages. "Reach up and grab onto the tree."

"Aye aye, Captain."

"You need to kiss me with that smart mouth."

What choice do I have when those lips of his make me weak?

It feels strange to look down at Austin from this angle. He's unbelievably strong.

His chest and arm muscles strain under the effort, but I couldn't convince him to put me down if I tried. And I don't want to.

The friction is intense. So much so that I can feel myself getting closer to coming with every slide. I grip his shaft as we move together, and he grinds out a curse,

I squeeze his middle with my thighs. His hands fondle my round cheeks, holding me in place.

My hard button rubs against his groin again and again. When Austin nudges the fabric of my bikini top aside with his face, he locks his mouth over one nipple. All it takes is one quick tease of his tongue combined with our shared friction, and I come apart in his arms. "Oh my god, holy shit, yes!" The release almost makes me forget to hang on, but Austin's a trooper.

The walls of my sex tighten around him, and I see in his eyes he's about to come.

Ever the gentleman, Austin warns me.

He's about to pull out, his face a question mark. It's true; we've not finished that conversation yet. But I give him my answer by clasping my legs tight, letting him know that I am not messing around. He can stay inside me. Release inside me. Put a baby in me, as he likes to say.

A grunt escapes his throat, and I see the exact moment it hits. He looks as if his memory has been wiped clean, his eyes slightly vacant for half a second. As his warm seed splashes into my core, I remind him where he is with an owning kiss. I drink in the low rumble of pleasure as my pussy milks every last drop from him.

"Sierra. Baby." And he's back.

I smile, kissing his face all over, whispering. "Captain. Where'd you go?"

As I kiss and kiss some more, he gently lifts me off him and sets me on the ground, helping me adjust my swimsuit to cover the essential bits.

He hugs me close. "I got lost for a moment there. You made me lose control of myself, Sierra."

I sigh and rest my head against his chest. "That was the first time I ever did it outside. Or standing up against a tree."

"I hope this Babymoon is full of firsts for you, Sierra."

"That was my first time without a condom."

"Me too. Feels different."

"Feels amazing."

"Buddy, I have a long list of firsts you can help me tick off."

"The Captain is at your service."

Chapter Twelve

Austin

To NOBODY'S SURPRISE, neither of us join Jax and Brooks on their foraging tour that afternoon.

We're already sweaty and too tangled up in the sheets to go anywhere.

The heated encounter at the palm tree continued into Sierra's hotel bed, where we followed that up with another round against the hotel room door and then in the bed until we both passed out from exhaustion.

My arm is asleep, and I'm dying of thirst, but I don't want to move. Once again, I am watching her sleep. This time, less fitfully. She still looks like an angel to me, but one with absolutely nothing troubling her mind.

In her sleep, she sighs contentedly and nestles back into me, her cute little butt pressing against my pelvis. I shouldn't wake her up, but my cock has other ideas. It stirs to life, hardens against her skin, and she feels it.

"Hmm. I'm surprised you're still able to do that," Sierra drawls in her sexy, sleepy voice.

Kissing down the back of her neck, Sierra shivers against me. I curl one arm around her waist and pull her right against me.

"I'm naked in bed with the mother of my future child. He's happy to get so much attention."

She giggles, and the vibration further eggs me on. I thrust against her, slide my hand down and cup her between her legs. Sierra sucks in a breath.

I whisper in her ear. "I have a secret."

"Oh, I don't like secrets."

"This is a nice one. I've been looking up online the most effective positions for getting pregnant. And you'll never guess."

"What?"

"It's one we haven't tried yet."

She sighs and rolls over to face me. "Look. I don't have the energy for reverse cowgirl right now or whatever it may be—"

I silence her with my kiss, communicating with my touches and lips that she'll not have to do a damn thing.

"Just lie back and let me handle it."

For me to be so hard after pleasing her just a short time ago is almost unthinkable. Yet with Sierra, my body only wants to worship her every moment of the day. A few short days ago, she was my drug, and I couldn't get enough. Now she's my sustenance. My everything.

I drag my hand up from her center to cup her face, administering sweet kisses over her face. Then, cupping her breasts, I slowly suckle at each nipple, thrilling at the sight of them going tight and needy for more. My mind pictures them full and rounded for the feeding of our child.

I slide my fingertips down her soft tummy to cup the

juncture between her thighs once again, marveling at Sierra's wetness. It's like we were made for each other. I roll over on top of her and cage her in with my arms, nestling between her legs.

"Ooh, missionary. You're a freak," she giggles.

She's joking, but I am a freak. She has no idea how long or how often I can get it in and keep it in.

Chapter Thirteen

Sierra

I KNOW this isn't just any regular ole missionary position as soon as Austin pins my wrists down above my head on the mattress. His gaze locks onto mine as he slides the tip in. Up until now, we've been fucking. Up against the tree, against the door, me mounting him and riding his cock like a freaking rodeo. But this is making love.

Once again, he enters me, but I know this time it's different. There's something different in his eyes this time. The frantic beast has calmed down, and now all I see is the real man inside—the firmness to my softness, the adventurer to my caution, the guardian of my heart.

Bit by bit, Austin reminds me of where I belong.

I arch upward to take it more, but he's giving it to me so slowly I'm forming tears in my eyes.

"Whose are you? Whose girl are you?"

"Yours," I whisper.

"Who are you making a baby with? Who's the daddy?"
My body aches for more. "You're the daddy. Please."
"Please, what?"
"Captain. Please, Captain."
He finally pushes in to the hilt, and though this is hardly our first time, I gasp at the sensation.

It's so good. Austin's so good. And not just good sex. He knows how to touch and tease and kiss. His body speaks to me and knows what I want. But more than that, I feel safe. Cared for. Cherished. Safe and protected.

I expect him to begin the delicious movements, but at first, he stays put, just letting me feel full of him. Austin nuzzles my neck. "Sierra. I…"

He trails off, and then I see why. His Adam's apple bobs up and down as he swallows.

"Don't bottle it up. Say what you need to say."

For a moment, I brace myself because I'm waiting for bad news. I'm preparing myself for him to tell me, even as he's seated inside me, that he's going to miss me. That this has been fun, this has been real, but…really? The son of a bitch is going to tell me goodbye while he's in the middle of a dicking?

His eyes are sad. "I don't want you to leave."

He's so choked up with feelings that I can't even be mad that he's trying to let me down gently. I can't be angry because, of course, this thing is going to run its course.

He has a life here. I have a life in the States. Our baby will be ours, and he will know his child, somehow. But really, this relationship can't continue like this.

I smile sadly back at him. "I wish I could stay in paradise forever."

"Do it. Stay with me."

I gasp. "Austin."

"Sierra, I love you. I don't want this to end. Not now, not a month from now, not when the baby comes. Never. I want you, and that's the end of the story. I love you, and I want to be with you, and I want to raise a baby with you. I want to put five more in you."

"Austin!" I giggle. "Five?"

He smiles and says breathlessly, "if that's what you want."

Tears flow out of my eyes and down to my temples. "But how do we…how do I … just how?"

Austin frees my wrists and cups my face, kissing my lips deeply, earnestly, then kisses away my tears.

"We figure it out. Together. Do you trust me?"

I nod my head.

He begins to move inside me, and I've never felt a close connection to anyone. Our gazes remain locked together. Austin covers my arms in his, and the weight of them, feeling him everywhere like a blanket, reassures me. Everything is going to be okay—more than okay. Everything is going to be extraordinary.

"It's not going to be easy," I say.

Austin doesn't seem to hear me as he pulls out slightly and drives back in, firmly, lovingly.

"As for me," he whispers, "I'm going to make it all as easy as possible. You don't have to worry about a thing."

"I've heard that somewhere before," I remark.

Our shared movements take on the familiar sensual rhythm, and all talking stops, replaced with moans, purrs, and pants.

Somewhere my phone rings, but I don't answer it. I know it's not Jax; she's with Brooks, and I can honestly say I feel good knowing she's spending time with him. Who knew my glamorous friend would fall for a shy naturalist who knows more about bugs than he knows about women? I'm relieved, actually.

As for me, all questions about how logical this plan is to stay on vacation forever, with Austin, fade into the background. All there is in this moment is him and me.

"It's the island way, sweetheart."

Epilogue

Sierra

Six months later

So, yeah. I stayed at The Pearl Crescent islands.

My slight baby bump and I have moved into Austin's house on Pearl Island to be close to a doctor.

I was perfectly fine with the idea of settling down on one of the smaller islands and hiring a midwife from one of the small mountain villages to help me deliver the baby, but Austin would not hear of it.

With everything that happened to Jax, I'm more than happy to take her and Brooks to the most remote section of The Pearl Crescent to live out our days. I shudder to think what would have happened to them if I had not, eventually, answered my phone when she had needed me most. While Austin and I were tangled up in bed, getting to know each other, I'd assumed that Jax and Brooks were falling in love in the jungle. Little did I know the dangers closing in on them.

To this day I still have to remind myself: "Everyone is fine. We're all safe now."

Jax and Brooks both side with Austin that I should deliver this baby on the big island. And I can't argue with that. Austin is a doting boyfriend and wants to protect me. Jax and Brooks are as good as family, and I know they'll be here to support us in whatever comes our way.

I've had to apply for permanent residence here. Because Austin wasn't born here, it's a whole process, but he's done an excellent job helping me navigate the system. And our child will have dual citizenship.

While my parents have threatened to cut me off, it doesn't much matter because the trust left to me by my grandparents will cover anything this baby needs. I offer to find a job, but Austin won't hear of it, at least not until I find something I like. What I want to do is volunteer.

Tonight, we're using his outdoor shower hidden in his overgrown backyard. It's a beautiful space, and I have big plans for it. He's rubbing a soapy loofah over my tummy when I'm oddly reminded of grooming horses.

"Oh, that reminds me. I saw something online about a therapist who uses donkeys for therapy. I might see if they need volunteers taking care of the animals."

Austin arches an eyebrow at me. "Me rubbing you down reminded you of that how? Wait, let me guess. Donkey grooming?"

I nod and giggle. "You know my number."

Austin runs the soft sponge over my breasts, which have grown much fuller since I've gotten pregnant. "No working or volunteering until after the baby's born. And only if you want to."

I pout. "But I want to now."

His eyes grow dark. "If you spend time with the donkeys, I'll never see you again."

"That's not true. I'll go whenever you have to work. I have nothing else to do around here but plan the wedding."

"My future wife likes to be busy taking care of everyone around her."

I wait for it, because I know what's next. And I get it. Austin drags the loofah down between my legs and gently swipes. I gasp slightly and reach my arms to hug his neck while balancing my foot on the shower bench.

"Nope. Have a seat. I'm going to take care of my wife."

The next second, I'm seated with my fingers gripping Austin's hair with his head between my legs. This happens whenever we shower together. And if we're home, neither of us showers alone.

His mouth devours my pussy, filling my entire body with so much sensation I can feel my spirit leave my body. When his lips find my clit, he gently nuzzles it, licking it until my thighs begin to tremble. He sucks it into his mouth, and I come apart.

"Austin!" I cry.

He answers with a grunt, and I laugh even as my body jerks through my intense release.

Minutes later, he feeds me ice cream while my legs are propped up in his lap.

I sigh. "You wanna chat about the guest list or baby names?"

He considers this. "Wedding guests. My brother in Santa Fe and his wife are coming."

"Right," I say, flipping through my planner. "I have them down."

Austin eyes me warily. "Have your parents responded yet?"

I wince. It's been months since I saw them when I flew back home to pack up my condo and told them the news that I found love in the middle of the South Pacific.

"No."

"Should we move the wedding to the States? Would that make them happy?"

I sigh and shake my head. "Nothing will make them happy unless I come home and take over the family business. So that's not happening. I'll keep trying, though. Sooner or later, they will realize they are about to be grandparents, and we won't be able to keep them away."

"I hope you're right. So let's mark them down as a yes just in case they have a last-minute change of heart."

"Jax and Brooks?"

I laugh. "If they ever come out of their love cocoon, then maybe," I say. "As they're the best man and best woman, let's plan on it."

Eventually, we move on to baby names.

I say, "If it's a boy, Kipling. If it's a girl, Jules."

Austin stares at me for a few beats. "So, your parents might be a more fun topic."

I swat him in the shoulder playfully.

"Fine, what do you suggest?"

He looks thoughtful. "Ralphie?"

"Come on!"

"Burke Belcher?"

"Oh my god, you can't stop thinking about that guy, can you?"

Austin attacks me about as roughly as he will allow himself to do with my new baby bump.

Careful not to put weight on my tum, he presses a hot, claiming kiss to my mouth.

"Still jealous even though it's your baby in me?"

He growls and nudges his knee in between my thighs, drawing it up deliciously.

"Mine. Always and forever."

"All I'll ever want is you and our baby, Captain."

Austin pulls me up onto his lap and crowds me against his chest, kissing my forehead. "You know what I think? I think it's time for a real babymoon."

I look at him skeptically and ask what he means.

"Now that you're pregnant, it's time for one last vacation together before the baby arrives. Anywhere you want to go. Name it. I'll fly us there."

"To Santa Fe. I want to meet your mom before the wedding."

He laughs and gives me a sweet ice cream kiss. "Family isn't exactly a vacation, babe."

Dabbing a spoon of ice cream on his nose then licking it off, I tell him the truth that he needs to know. "Everywhere is a vacation with you, Captain."

Epilogue

Five years later

Austin

Sierra, Jax, Brooks, and I have started a tradition in which we celebrate our wedding anniversaries together.

In earlier years, the four of us plus my and Sierra's son, Kiran, were content with a thatched-roof hut in the remote Severed Key. Those were simpler times. But now, between our two families, we may be causing a population explosion on The Pearl Crescent islands.

Kiran has been joined by a sister, Sidney. The four-year-old and the two-year-old are too fearless and need constant supervision. For us to feel relaxed and enjoy a true vacation, we've rented out a villa at DragonZone, the family-friendly sector of Cerulean Resort.

As for Jax and Brooks, their two boys, Lief and Kai, are even more of a handful.

We're raising four wild island children who are expert swimmers, fearless climbers, and adept paddle-boarders. The DragonZone staff has their work cut out for them.

On this day, we four adults have parked ourselves at the beachfront tiki bar not far from where the kids are making sandcastles with a bunch of other visitors and resort staffers.

Understandably, Sierra feels the need to turn and check on the tiny Sidney, who's as likely as not to wander away from the group.

I reach over squeeze her hand. "Do you ever regret not moving back to the States? It's not too late."

Sierra cuts her eyes over to Jax and Brooks, who no doubt will live out their days here on the islands. Going back may never be safe for her, but especially not for Brooks.

My question must have reminded her of something, because she takes a moment to send a text. "Just sending some photos of the kids to my parents and to your mom."

I squeeze her hand again, because I know that her decision to stay here was not received well by her family. Although they've warmed up to her because of the kids — and let's face it; kids are a great buffer for judgmental family — the distance has meant that the kids don't receive enough traditional grandparent time.

"Here's the way I see it. Your mom is not made of money, and yet she visits as often as she's able to save up the money, refusing any help. My parents are retired, with oodles of money. They could retire here or visit as much as they want, but they seldom do," Sierra says. "Life is all about who and what you make time for. Traditional doesn't work for me. Raising our kids almost one hundred percent outdoors, with an entire island full of people looking out for them, as total nonconformists who can grow up to be whatever they want? It far outweighs any traditional family set up. We take our chances and we don't look back."

My heart swells with love for this woman. I fell in love with her the instant we met, and though I tried to resist, she taught me to let go of the stranglehold I had over my emotions.

Sierra sees the strange look on my face; I can't hide it when I'm getting choked up, thinking of how we've had nothing but time to get to know each other these past few years. I don't take for granted a single second. "What's on your mind, babe?"

"What's on my mind is how I was never sure I'd have a wife, a family and real friends. Everyone in my life up until I met you was already married with kids. Way ahead of where I wanted to be. But this place is full of found families of all different backgrounds," I comment. "I just never thought I'd find mine."

THE END

THANK YOU FOR READING BABYMOON! If you enjoyed this short story, please visit my website for links to my Amazon page where you can find lots more titles to read. Follow me there to keep up with my latest releases. Or, just say hello! Turn the page and find out where to track me down on social media and email, or sign up for my mailing list to be the first to know about upcoming projects.

The Naughty Yachties series

Shipped

Secret Baby on Board

Wrecked

Decked

Roped

The Roadside Attractions series

Roadside Attraction

Claiming Fate

Falling into Fate

Fate's Dark Shadows

Rode Hard

Crash into Me

Snowed Under

The Homemade Heat series

Judge Me

Cake Walk

Hand-Tossed

Chef's Kiss

Bite Me

And plenty more on my website at authorabbyknox.com

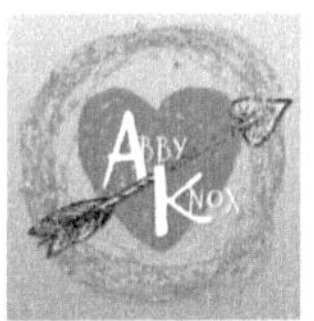

About the Author

Abby Knox writes feel-good, high-heat romance that she herself would want to read. Readers have described her stories as quirky, sexy, adorable, and hilarious. All of that adds up to Abby's overall goal in life: to be kind and to have fun!

Abby's favorite tropes include: Forced proximity, opposites attract, grumpy/sunshine, age gap, boss/employee, fated mates/insta-love, and more. Abby is heavily influenced by Buffy the Vampire Slayer, Gilmore Girls, and LOST. But don't worry, she won't ever make you suffer like Luke & Lorelai.

If any or all of that connects with you, then you came to the right place.

Say hello at authorabbyknox@gmail.com

Find all important links, and sign up for my newsletter, at authorabbyknox.com